NORMAN

Based on a true story

By Heather Young

Illustrations by Ramir Quintana
Edited by Lisa Tabachnick Hotta

Portion of the proceeds of this book will go to:

Heaven Can Wait Equine Rescue - www.heavencanwaitequinerescue.org

Heaven Can Wait Equine Rescue is located in Cameron, Ontario, Canada. This Equine Rescue was started by Claire Malcolm in 1997 to help save horses and ponies from slaughter, and take in any unwanted horse or pony and find them a new, loving home.

HCW has found loving new homes for over 1000++ equines in the past 15 years (& has even helped find new homes for a few donkeys, pigs, goats, cats & dogs along the way!).

AND

LongRun Thoroughbred Retirement Society - www.longrunretirement.com

LongRun Thoroughbred Retirement Society, a registered charity whose offices are located on the backstretch of Woodbine Racetrack in Toronto, attempts to provide as many of Ontario's thoroughbred racehorses as possible with a dignified retirement once their days at the races are over by fostering, rehabilitating and retraining them prior to their adoptions into loving, permanent homes.

In addition, LongRun attempts to educate the racing community and the general public as to the merits of this program and the beauty, athleticism and intelligence of the horses who run for our pleasure

Charity Number: 87761 9528 RR0001

To order additional copies of this book, contact:
Xlibris Corporation
1-888-795-4274
www.Xlibris.com
Orders@Xlibris.com

This book is dedicated to:

Norman who constantly amazes me at his willingness to always give 100% of his heart in everything he does.

To anyone who has been told they can't

Acknowledgements

Jim: Thanks for always being there to support me and catching me when I fall

Donna, Tammy and Ron: I am lucky to have you in my life. Thanks for putting up with me

Kristine, Monica and Leona: Thanks for all the laughs, late nights, Senators games and the heartfelt talks

Stacey: Thanks for always being you and for that laugh that is so contagious

Alex and Chelsea: For making my family complete

Lisa, my editor: thank you for you guidance and help

Staff of Foxhunter: Thank you for your support and the great care you took of Norman.

Todd Owens: Thank you for showing me a different way of communicating with Norman and helping him to adapt to his new reality

There once was a very special horse named Norman who lived on a beautiful farm with his friends. Norman and his friends loved to run in the soft grass, roll in the dirt and play tag in the green fields.

Each week, all of the horses, including Norman, waited excitedly for Saturday. It was on Saturdays that the children came for their riding lessons. The horses would follow alongside the fence as the cars, that carried the children, drove up the farm's driveway toward the riding arena.

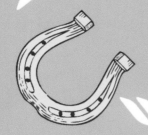

The little girl who rode Norman was named Prudence. The two of them always had so much fun together. Prudence would take her time grooming Norman before each ride and she always brought him his favourite treat - a large, orange carrot.

During the lessons, Norman and Prudence ran and jumped over all of the fences in the arena as others stopped to watch and smile. Everywhere they went people commented on what a good team they were.

After they finished their lesson, Norman and Prudence would go out to the field, lay down in the grass under their favourite tree and watch the clouds go by until Prudence's mother came to pick her up to take her home.

But, things did not always go perfectly for Norman and Prudence. One morning in June, Norman woke up with a very sore right eye. Farmer Sue noticed that something was wrong. Concerned, she helped Norman onto the horse trailer and drove him into town to see the special animal doctor, Dr. Jim.

Dr. Jim looked at Norman's eye and did not like what he saw. He told Norman and Farmer Sue that because of an infection Norman would lose his eyesight in that eye. He said Norman would have to wear an eye patch to protect the eye from hurting against the light.

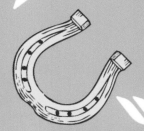

As the doctor placed the eye patch on Norman, he explained that Norman would no longer be able to jump fences because he wouldn't see things in the same way and his balance would be off. Norman was so sad to hear the news because he loved jumping and he was afraid he would disappoint Prudence. What if Prudence decided to switch to a horse who could jump? Norman would miss Prudence terribly.

Farmer Sue helped Norman get back into the trailer for the ride home. When they returned to the farm and the trailer door was opened, Norman timidly stepped off the ramp wearing his new eye patch. Everyone came out to welcome him home but no one was happier to see him than Prudence. She ran up to her big brown horse, stood on her tippy toes and gave him a kiss right on the nose.

The very next day, Norman, determined to continue their riding lessons and prove the doctor wrong, went out into the field and tried jumping over anything he could. But he only tripped and fell down. For the rest of the week, Norman tried and tried, only to keep falling down.

Right before Saturday's lesson, Norman went out into the field, closed his eyes and made a wish. He then ran as fast as he could towards the jump while his friends cheered him on.

Norman held his breath, leaped into the air and, when he opened his eyes, to his surprise he was standing on the other side of the jump! He made it! But could he do it with Prudence on his back?

On Saturday, when the children began to arrive, Norman was nervous but he was also really looking forward to seeing Prudence. He was still worried that she would choose another horse to ride. He watched as Prudence opened the farm gate and walk into the field. To Norman's relief she walked right up to him and gave him a big hug, a carrot and led him out of his paddock towards the barn.

They were having a fantastic lesson, like nothing had changed. Prudence knew in her heart that Norman could still make it over all of the jumps, he just needed to believe in himself. To prove to Norman that he could do it, she turned towards a fence, nudged Norman on with a soft whisper, "You can do this Norman" and over the jump they went.

When Norman and Prudence landed gracefully on the other side, he was so proud of himself that he whinnied loudly for all to hear. The crowd who had gathered around the arena clapped and cheered for the big brown horse and the little girl who helped him get his confidence back. Prudence smiled, gave Norman a big pat on his neck and said, "I knew you could do it."

And today . . .

Norman and Prudence continue to ride and compete together. Norman wears his eye patch everywhere they go, winning many ribbons and awards. But, no award is as special as the bond that exists between the two friends and knowing that you can do anything as long as you believe in yourself... and have a good friend to remind you when you forget.

The End.

CPSIA information can be obtained
at www.ICGtesting.com
Printed in the USA
LVHW070919200120
644146LV00016B/2119